S0-BSN-149

BRODART, CO.

Printed in U.S.A.

LITTLE HOUSE

Caroline #5

# A New Little Cabin

ADAPTED FROM THE CAROLINE YEARS BOOKS BY
## Maria D. Wilkes

ILLUSTRATED BY
## Doris Ettlinger

HarperTrophy®
*A Division of HarperCollinsPublishers*

FREEPORT LIBRARY ASSOC.
428 MARKET ST.
FREEPORT, PA. 16229

37969

*Adaptation by Heather Henson.*

HarperCollins®, ☙®, Little House®, Harper Trophy®, and
The Caroline Years™ are trademarks of HarperCollins Publishers Inc.

A New Little Cabin
Text adapted from *Little Town at the Crossroads*, text copyright 1997 by
HarperCollins Publishers Inc.; *Little Clearing in the Woods*, text copyright 1998
by HarperCollins Publishers Inc.
Illustrations by Doris Ettlinger
Illustrations copyright © 2001 by Renée Graef
Copyright © 2001 by HarperCollins Publishers
All rights reserved. No part of this book may be used or reproduced
in any manner whatsoever without written permission except in the case
of brief quotations embodied in critical articles and reviews. Printed in
the United States of America. For information address HarperCollins
Children's Books, a division of HarperCollins Publishers,
1350 Avenue of the Americas, New York, NY 10019.
www.harperchildrens.com

Library of Congress Cataloging-in-Publication Data
Wilkes, Maria D.
   A new little cabin / adapted from the Caroline years books by Maria D.
Wilkes ; illustrated by Doris Ettlinger.—1st ed.
      p.       cm.—(Little house chapter book)
   "Caroline #5."
   Summary: When Caroline Quiner and her family are forced to move from
Brookfield further west, Caroline, who will become the mother of Laura
Ingalls Wilder, does her part as they settle in and make a new home.
   ISBN 0-06-028554-0 (lib. bdg.) — ISBN 0-06-442109-0 (pbk.)
   1. Ingalls, Caroline Lake Quiner—Juvenile fiction.   [1. Ingalls, Caroline Lake
Quiner—Fiction.   2. Wilder, Laura Ingalls, 1867–1957—Family—Fiction.
3. Moving, Household—Fiction.   4. Family life—Wisconsin—Fiction.
5. Frontier and pioneer life—Wisconsin—Fiction.   6. Wisconsin—Fiction.]
1. Ettlinger, Doris, ill.   II. Title.   III. Series.
PZ7.W648389 Ne   2001                                               00-39717
[Fic]—dc21

Typography by Carla Weise
1   2   3   4   5   6   7   8   9   10
❖
First Harper Trophy Edition, 2001

# Contents

# CHAPTER 1

# The Letter

Caroline lived in a little frame house in Brookfield, Wisconsin. She had two sisters, Martha and Eliza, and three brothers, Joseph, Henry, and little Thomas.

One day Mother told them she had heard that a letter had arrived at Mr. Porter's General Store. But Mother was too busy to go to town. And she needed Martha and Joseph to stay home and help with chores. So she said Caroline could go with Henry as he took Hog to town. She told Caroline to take Thomas along too.

"But Caroline is only seven years old! You're going to let her fetch something as important as a letter?" Martha asked in a huff. She was only two years older than Caroline but acted like she knew everything.

"Caroline knows the value of a letter, Martha," Mother said. "I expect she'll have little trouble picking it up and bringing it home safely. Am I correct, Caroline?"

"Yes, ma'am," Caroline nodded importantly with a sideways glance at Martha. "I'll be very careful."

As soon as the frame house was swept and tidied, Caroline took Thomas's hand.

"You stay with your sister, Thomas. No running off," Mother said. And then she turned to Caroline. "Be mindful of your brother, Caroline."

"I will, ma'am," Caroline promised.

Outside the sky was a clear blue, but the air was chilly. Caroline hugged herself against the cold. She was glad she was wearing her heaviest long-sleeved dress.

Henry was already waiting. He waved and called, "Let's go!" as he led Hog onto the road.

As they neared the crossroads of town, the road suddenly grew crowded with men

and boys driving their hogs toward wagons lined up on the main road. Henry hurried Hog toward the wagon to eat as Caroline and Thomas made their way carefully to the general store.

"Well, good morning to you, Miss Quiner!" Mr. Porter called as Caroline stepped inside. "And to you too, lad," he added, nodding his shiny bald head at Thomas.

"Good morning, Mr. Porter." Caroline smiled up at the grocer. "Mother sent us to fetch a letter for her, sir."

"Ah, yes," Mr. Porter said, setting his pencil down on the counter. "I'll get it for you right away."

While Mr. Porter searched for the letter, Caroline gazed up and down the shelves. She always loved coming to the general store. There were so many things to see: dishes and spices and pretty cloth and lace. And jars filled with candy. Her mouth watered as she looked at the two glass jars right in front of her. They held glistening sticks of peppermint and round wintergreen candies.

Thomas was looking at the same jars.

"I want one," he said.

"Me too," Caroline whispered. "But we can't have any."

"Why?" Thomas wanted to know.

"Because they don't belong to us," Caroline said, feeling very grown up. "And they cost money, besides. Now shush, Thomas."

"Here you are, young lady." Mr. Porter returned and slid a thin brown envelope over the edge of the crowded counter. "It looks like this one has traveled all the way from back East."

"Thank you, sir," Caroline said, taking the letter in her hands. She looked at the sprawling black script. The letters were curvy and connected, and she couldn't read one word.

"Please send my greetings to your mother." Mr. Porter smiled down at her.

"I will," Caroline promised. "Thank you, sir, and good-bye."

As soon as they were outside again, Caroline took her little brother's hand and began to walk quickly. Henry was staying in town, and Caroline wanted to get home as fast as she could to see what was inside the letter.

"Come on now, Thomas," she said.

Thomas hurried along beside Caroline, trying his best to keep up. When they arrived at the frame house, Mother was alone, placing the top crust of a pie.

"Goodness, Thomas," Mother said with a laugh. " Your cheeks are as round and red as apples!"

"Caroline goes fast," Thomas said. "I go fast, too!" he added proudly. He looked at the pie. "Now eat!"

"Soon," Mother promised, and then she turned to Caroline. "Did you get the letter?"

"Yes, Mother," Caroline smiled proudly. "It's right here, safe and sound!"

"Good for you, Caroline," Mother praised. She rubbed her hands on her apron and wiped away the flour and dough stuck between her fingers.

"I go outside!" Thomas said, bouncing up and down in place.

"Go ahead," Mother agreed as Thomas raced for the door. "But don't go any farther than the barn."

"Mr. Porter says it's from back East," Caroline said, handing the letter to Mother. Maybe it was from her grandparents in Boston.

"He's right," Mother said. She looked at the writing. "But it's not from Boston."

Mother slid the knife through the edge of the envelope and pulled out a single sheet of paper.

"Who's it from?" Caroline asked.

Mother didn't answer. Her eyes darted from one line to the next. As she read, her hands began to tremble a little. Caroline knew that whatever was in the letter was not good news.

"Please, Mother," Caroline asked quietly. "What's happened?"

Caroline knew she shouldn't ask any more questions. But Mother had the same look of fear and worry on her face that

 8

Caroline had seen only once before: the terrible day when Uncle Elisha told them that Father's ship had been lost at sea and he was never coming home again. That had been two years ago.

"Please, Mother," Caroline begged. "Say what's wrong!"

Mother was silent a moment. Then she knelt down in front of Caroline.

"We are going to have to leave our house, Caroline," Mother said.

"I don't understand," Caroline cried.

"Years ago your father and I fell on some very hard times." Mother spoke very slowly. "We were forced to sell our land to a Mr. Woods. Mr. Woods didn't want to live on the land himself, so he let us stay here for a small amount of money. But now Mr. Woods's sister and her family are coming to Brookfield this spring. They plan to live on this land. We'll have to find another place to live."

Caroline looked at the piece of folded paper. She wanted to tear it into tiny pieces and make sure that what Mother was telling her would not come true.

"You mustn't worry, Caroline," Mother said. "I've been planning for this day. I've been taking on extra sewing jobs from folks in town and saving the money so we can buy land somewhere else."

"In Brookfield?" Caroline asked.

"Well, we need enough land to raise a good crop and some livestock," Mother said. "I don't imagine that we can get that kind of land in Brookfield for the amount of money I'm able to pay."

Caroline dropped her head. She thought of her friends, Anna and Elsa. She thought of her favorite neighbors, the

Carpenters. She thought of the town and the general store and the bubbling creek where she picked berries and wildflowers. She looked around the snug little frame house. She shut her eyes as tight as she could, but the tears came anyway.

"Dear Caroline," Mother said, pulling her into a warm hug. "You mustn't cry. We don't have to go anywhere until spring. That's six whole months from now!"

Mother smiled down at Caroline. Her voice was firm.

"Now promise me, not a word about this to anyone until I've told them myself. Promise me."

"I promise," Caroline whispered. Usually she liked to share a secret with Mother. It made her feel special. But this secret did not make her feel good at all. It only made her feel very, very sad.

# CHAPTER 2

# Making Plans

Caroline hardly spoke during dinner and supper. She stayed quiet as she worked at the sewing table with Mother and Martha and Eliza before bedtime.

Martha hummed as she clicked her knitting needles together. Eliza carefully watched Mother's expert stitches so she could practice her own later.

Joseph was stoking the fire, and Henry sat cross-legged on the floor in front of the hearth, carving a block of wood.

Suddenly Martha stopped humming.

"Who was the letter from today, Mother?" she asked. "You never told us at supper."

Caroline studied the verse she was stitching on her sampler. She didn't dare look up. She knew that Martha might see in her eyes that she knew Mother's secret.

Mother took a deep breath.

"The letter was from Pennsylvania," she answered. "From a man named Michael Woods. It wasn't good news."

Joseph stopped poking the fire. "What's happened, Mother?" he asked.

Mother set down her sewing. She looked around the room at each face. In a calm and steady voice, she told them what she had told Caroline earlier.

"You mean we have to go away from here?" Martha gasped as she dropped her knitting needles on her lap.

"Yes, Martha," Mother said. "And I

don't yet know where we'll go. I have saved some money to buy land, but if we choose to purchase it here, we'll likely get too little to farm and raise animals. We may need to go farther west. Land will be cheaper there."

Martha stuttered, "But how can we leave . . ."

"Charlie?" Henry finished, his eyes twinkling. Martha especially liked Charlie Carpenter, and the boys always teased her about it. Martha's face turned a bright pink.

"Oh, Martha!" Henry continued. "It doesn't matter where our diggings are! Charlie and his folks will come visit. Heck, they might even move along with us, it's such an adventure!"

"There's the money we made from shooting pigeons, Mother," Joseph said.

"Mr. Carleton owes us ten dollars and fifty-six cents. It could help buy land."

"You bet!" Henry agreed.

"Thank you, boys," Mother said proudly.

"I don't have any money," Thomas burst out from the floor, where he was stacking wooden blocks.

"Well, I don't have much, either."

15

Mother laughed. "So wherever we go, it will have to be a place where we can get a fair amount of land for a good price."

"When will we go?" Eliza asked.

"In the spring," Mother replied. Then she said in a cheerful voice, "But enough of these glum faces. Henry is right. We should think of this as an adventure. A chance to start over with our own land, land that can't be taken away. We'll plant wheat as well as corn and eventually raise our own livestock. You're all getting old enough to help with such big and important chores."

"We could raise some geese," Joseph spoke up.

"That's a fine idea." Mother smiled.

"Don't forget chickens," Eliza chimed in.

"And bees!" Henry cried. "We could raise us some bees and eat all their honey!"

"Maybe they won't have a schoolhouse in this new place, and we'll never have to go back to school!" Martha grinned. She did not like school as much as Caroline did.

"*I* hope there's a school," Caroline spoke up finally.

"Well, if there isn't one, you'll have all your lessons with me, in the new cabin that we build," Mother said in a firm voice.

For the rest of the evening, Caroline listened as her brothers and sisters talked about new plans with Mother. Caroline knew moving would be an adventure. But she still ached when she thought about leaving the home she loved.

# CHAPTER 3

# Saying Good-bye

The months seemed to pass in no time at all. In the first cold days of February, Uncle Elisha came from Milwaukee. He and Mother traveled thirty miles west to a town named Concord. There Mother purchased a log cabin with forty acres of land.

When she returned, the family stayed in Brookfield a little while longer. But once the days turned warmer, Mother stopped the sewing and mending that had kept her busy in the evenings all fall and winter. She began to pack up the family's belongings.

Then one day Uncle Elisha came again and began to help load everything into his wagon. Mr. Carpenter drove his wagon over as well. He and Charlie would be coming along after all. But they would only stay a few weeks to help Caroline's family settle into their new place.

As the Quiners got ready to leave, friends and neighbors visited to say their good-byes. Caroline said her saddest farewell to her best friend, Anna.

At last everything was nearly packed up into the two wagons. Caroline would ride in Uncle Elisha's wagon with Mother, Thomas, Martha, and Eliza. The wagons were so full, Joseph and Henry would have to take turns walking and riding with Mr. Carpenter and Charlie.

Caroline was just about to climb in beside her sisters when she suddenly remembered something.

"I forgot to remind Henry to take my chickens!" she cried.

Taking care of the chickens had always been Caroline's special chore. Now she rushed over to Mr. Carpenter's wagon.

"Henry!" she called. "Don't forget the hens."

"Don't worry," Henry called back. "Every one of them sqawkers is packed already."

Caroline watched as Henry swung a hay-filled mattress up to Joseph. The wagon was packed full with sacks and barrels and tables and trunks. There were two reed hampers that held all their clothes. There was Mother's butter churn and the three large barrels of salt pork, flour, and corn meal. A washtub rested in the center of the wagon. Inside it was a collection of iron kettles and the leftover beans, peas, and potatoes from last fall's harvest. Beside the tub four wooden chairs rested upside down on top of a square oak table.

"You didn't pile anything on the hens, did you?" Caroline asked.

"If you think I want to find a gunnysack

full of dead chickens when we get to Concord, you're mighty mistaken, little Brownbraid," Henry said, laughing.

Little Brownbraid was Caroline's special nickname. Father had given it to her because of the one long braid she always wore down her back.

"Now you better get back to Uncle Elisha's wagon," Henry continued. "We're 'bout ready to go."

Caroline let out a little sigh. As she trudged back toward the wagon, she took one last look past the garden and barn. She could just see the green marshes where her favorite yellow blossoms had begun to appear. She wanted to run into the field and pick a bouquet, but she knew there wasn't time.

Instead she thought about all the favorite places she had visited that morning: the barn, the henhouse, the garden, the old oak tree that tapped her bedroom window as she fell asleep on windy nights. Her throat suddenly felt tight.

"You almost didn't get back in time," Martha scolded.

Caroline silently climbed up and sat down beside Eliza. The girls were riding on a narrow plank of wood that had been fastened across the center of the wagon.

"Henry has the hens, and I finished all my good-byes," Caroline said.

Just then Mother came out of the house with Thomas running behind her.

"The sweeping's done, and that's the last of it," she called.

"We have everything packed now," Joseph told her.

Mother nodded, and Caroline could see that her eyes were bright.

"Into the wagon, boys, and we'll pull foot!" Mr. Carpenter's cheerful voice suddenly rang out in the crisp morning air. "There's a wagonload of work awaiting us at the end of the trail!"

Mother smiled, and Caroline felt better. She was glad Mr. Carpenter was coming with them. He always made everything seem jolly.

As Mr. Carpenter and Uncle Elisha climbed into the wagons, Joseph let out a loud whistle. Wolf, their large gray dog, bounded out from the barn, leaping and barking.

"You're certain you have everything now, Charlotte?" Mr. Carpenter called.

Mother nodded again. "And you're certain Sarah doesn't mind us borrowing you for a few weeks, Benjamin?" she asked.

"She wouldn't have it any other way,"

Mr. Carpenter answered warmly. "Now let's get started."

Uncle Elisha lifted the yoke and chain. "Move out now, fellas!" he shouted to the oxen, and the wagon pitched forward.

"Sit close to each other, girls," Mother said over her shoulder. "The road promises to be bumpy ahead."

Caroline braced herself against Eliza and glanced back one last time.

The frame house, the barn, the old oak, and leafy maples grew smaller and smaller as the wagons rattled along. In just a few minutes, Caroline could no longer see the only home she had ever known.

FREEPORT LIBRARY ASSOC.
428 MARKET ST.
FREEPORT, PA. 16229

37909

# CHAPTER 4

# Walking Trees

"Ouch!" Caroline cried as Eliza's head banged into her shoulder.

"I can't help it!" Eliza complained. "I wish we could get off this wagon right now!"

"I wish we could go back home," Caroline said under her breath. She gripped the side of the wagon, struggling to stay on the seat as they lurched back and forth along the rutted road.

Martha leaned across Eliza and pinched Caroline's arm.

"Don't be such a fusspot," she scolded. Then she turned to Eliza. "Sit as close to me as you can so the wagon won't toss you around so much. Uncle Elisha says it's at least three days to Concord. No sense complaining when we've barely made it through one day."

Caroline stared ahead silently. She knew Martha was right, but she wouldn't admit it. She hated when Martha acted so grown up.

The wind was turning cold and daylight was fading. Caroline reached deep into her coat pockets and squeezed the two potatoes that had kept her hands warm since they had left Brookfield.

"My potatoes are as cold as I am," she said in a quiet voice. She knew she was complaining again, but she couldn't help it. She tucked her hands beneath the

heavy quilt covering her legs.

"Mine are, too," Martha admitted. "The trees are walking much faster now than when we left this morning. The faster they walk, the colder it gets, I think."

Thomas clapped and bounced on the seat between Mother and Uncle Elisha.

"The trees are walking!" he cried.

"Trees don't walk, silly," Eliza said, but then she asked, "Do they, Caroline?"

"None that I ever saw," Caroline answered. She looked around. The wagon was surrounded by sprawling branches and budding leaves. As the wagon moved forward, it did seem like the trees were moving while the wagon stayed in its place. Caroline closed her eyes, and when she opened them, the trees stood still again as the wagon jolted past.

Suddenly a series of shrieks and whinnies screeched through the air. Caroline whirled around to see Mr. Carpenter's wagon tilt sharply into a deep rut. Mr. Carpenter quickly slid to the other side of the wagon beside Henry, but it was too late. The wagon kept tilting. Then the wheels collapsed beneath all the weight.

Mr. Carpenter and Henry and every-thing in the wagon were tossed out onto the ground. One of the black horses fell and lay kicking its bony legs furiously in the air. The other stood stamping at the earth.

"Whoa!" Uncle Elisha called to his team and jumped off the wagon. Caroline followed after Mother and Martha.

Mr. Carpenter was already up and rushing to pull the black horse to its feet. Caroline watched as he unbridled the team. He patted their flanks and talked to them, trying to calm them down.

"I'm afraid Henry may be hurt," Mother said in a worried voice.

Caroline dashed around to the other side of the wagon. Joseph and Charlie were kneeling beside Henry, who was sprawled on his back, cradling Mother's

 30

mahogany clock in his arms. Barrels and crates, bulging sacks, and a bundle of quilts tied with heavy twine had been tossed to the ground beside him.

"Are you all right, Henry?" Mother knelt down and gently stroked his brow. "Does anything feel broken?"

Henry shook his head. "Got the wind knocked out of me, is all," he said, and sat up. "I saved the clock," he added with a grin.

"Thank you." Mother smiled. She took the clock from his hands. "Now sit still for a moment."

"Are you hurt?" Martha asked Charlie and Joseph. They had been walking beside the wagon. "Your clothes are all dirty."

"That's what we get for diving out of the way," Charlie said, and grinned. He wiped the mud from his face and then went to help his father with the horses.

Joseph said his shoulder was sore, but that Henry and Mr. Carpenter had gotten the worst of it.

"This wheel has taken a beating," Mr. Carpenter said grimly from the other side of the wagon. "It's cracked but good and will need fixing before it can handle such a heavy load again."

He stood up and glanced at the sky. His face looked worried.

"It's near dark," he said after a while. "We'll stay here tonight and make camp. I'll have the wagon wheel fixed by morning."

Caroline looked around at the shadowy woods. She had never slept outdoors before.

"Let's get the wagon upright and take the wheel off," Uncle Elisha suggested.

Caroline helped her brothers and

sisters take their belongings out. As Mr. Carpenter and Uncle Elisha worked on the wagon, the boys gathered kindling to start a fire.

"Please come help me find the bake oven and some food to cook," Mother told Caroline.

"Yes, ma'am," Caroline answered. This was the first time she would ever help Mother cook over an open fire. And it was the first time she'd sleep on a wagon floor beneath the dark night sky. Caroline knew the boys thought this was a big adventure, but for her, home had never seemed so far away.

# CHAPTER 5

# Wolves

Soon the boys had built a roaring fire. Caroline helped Mother cook beans and corn bread. The beans came from out of a can that had traveled all the way from Boston. Caroline's grandparents had sent several cans in a trunk last Christmas. Caroline was hungry, and everything tasted extra good.

After supper everyone sat around the cozy fire. Mr. Carpenter told stories, and Caroline and Henry watched for shooting stars.

When it was time for bed, Mother told the girls to sleep in their warm clothes and coats and wrap themselves tightly in their quilts. Caroline and her sisters would sleep in Uncle Elisha's wagon with Mother. The boys would sleep with Mr. Carpenter and Uncle Elisha beside the fire.

As Caroline followed Martha and Eliza to the wagon, she listened to all the strange night sounds. A pair of hoot owls were calling out *Hoo! Hoo!* from the trees. Somewhere off in the distance, a wolf howled its mournful cry.

"Do you suppose there are any bears around here, Mr. Ben?" Caroline asked as Mr. Carpenter helped her into the wagon. Caroline and her brothers and sisters called Mr. Carpenter Mr. Ben.

"Too much starlight for any bears to come around tonight," Mr. Carpenter said.

35

"And if there is a frisky bear out there somewhere, he'll have to get past me first!"

Caroline felt better. She knew that Mr. Carpenter would keep them safe. As she snuggled in close to Eliza on the wagon bed, she stared up at the twinkling black sky above. There were so many stars. She tried to count them all, but she must have fallen asleep. The next thing she knew she was being shaken awake.

"Caroline! Caroline!" Martha was calling urgently.

Caroline opened her eyes and leaned up on her elbows.

"What's wrong?" she asked.

"The howls—they're coming closer!" Martha whispered.

Caroline held her breath and listened. The shrill, piercing cries of the wolves

 36

rang out in all directions. It sounded like they were all around the wagon.

"What's happened?" Mother asked sleepily.

"Listen," Caroline cried. "It's wolves! We have to get Mr. Ben. He'll keep them away."

"We shouldn't leave the wagon. We don't know where the wolves are," Mother said.

Caroline stared out into the darkness. She thought she saw yellow eyes darting in and out of the shadows. She opened her mouth to scream, but no sound came out. Instead she heard loud barking and saw Wolf bounding across the grass, leaping and snapping madly.

"Wolf!" Caroline cried. "Get Mr. Ben! He's there by the campfire. Go!"

"Run, Wolf!" Martha called.

In a flash, Mr. Carpenter and the boys were beside the wagon. They were holding tree limbs set afire.

"Take one girl each," Mr. Carpenter shouted. "Get them back to the fire and wait for me there!"

Henry took Eliza in his arms, and Joseph reached for Caroline. He pulled her to the fire. Martha followed close behind.

Mr. Carpenter and Uncle Elisha shouted and waved their flaming sticks at the wolves as Mother climbed down from the wagon with Thomas in her arms.

When they were all together, Mr. Carpenter had the boys pull out every long stick they could find from the fire. They gave two sticks to Mother and one each to Caroline and Martha. Mr. Carpenter told them to wave the burning sticks around in the air.

"Be careful," Mother warned Caroline. "Use both hands and keep the fire far away from your body."

"Whirl it around and make circles in the air, like this," Mr. Carpenter said, spinning his fire branch around and around.

Caroline held onto her burning stick so tightly the lumps and grooves in the bark dug into her skin. Little by little, she was able to move the stick, swirling it in small circles that gradually grew bigger and bigger.

"Shout! Everybody!" Mr. Carpenter urged. "As loud and angry as you can!"

Ever since she was a little girl, Caroline had been told that ladies never raised their voices. But now she shouted as loud as she could. She yelled and whooped and hollered. She danced around the blazing

fire with her family. Wolf bounded from side to side in front of Caroline, barking angrily.

By the time Caroline had burned through three sticks, she could no longer see a single pair of yellow eyes. The howls had disappeared as well.

"I reckon we've seen the last of that pack for a while," Mr. Carpenter tossed his burned tree stub into the fire and sighed heavily. Then he patted Wolf on the back. "Good work, old boy."

Even though the wolves were gone, Mr. Carpenter said that they should all sleep close to the fire for the rest of the night.

Caroline brought her quilt from the wagon. Once more she snuggled close to Eliza and Martha. The ground was cold, but the fire was warm. When she closed her eyes, Caroline could still see shadows of the flames and feel the safe, soothing heat on her cheeks. Mother began to sing a lullaby, and slowly Caroline drifted back to sleep.

# CHAPTER 6

# Clearing in the Woods

For three more nights, as the wagons traveled west, Caroline slept on the ground near the fire. She missed her nightgown and her soft straw mattress. She did not like how her dress and shawl and hair always smelled like smoke. She longed for a bath. But she dared not complain.

Finally the wagons came to a thick forest. Uncle Elisha said that they only had a mile to go. At last they would see their new home.

But the going was slow. There were so many trees that the wagons had to wind back and forth around them. Thin rays of sunshine fell here and there, but when Caroline looked up, leaves seemed to cover the whole sky.

"There's a clearing up ahead!" Joseph suddenly called.

"That's our land then," Mother cried. "We've arrived!"

"May we please run ahead, Mother?" Caroline asked.

"Go," Mother said, laughing, "but stay clear of the wagons."

Caroline took Eliza's hand and pulled her through piles of leaves toward the glowing light at the edge of the forest. They burst into the clearing, then stopped.

There, in a circle of sunlight completely surrounded by trees, sat a tiny log house. Dark rectangles stared out where a door and window should have been. A pile of logs and a wooden barrel rested against one side of the house. A stone chimney nestled on the other. Behind the house sat a small privy and part of a rail fence.

Caroline had never seen such a sad, lonely place.

"There's no door." Eliza's small voice echoed in the quiet.

"Or windowpanes, either," Martha said, coming up behind her.

"It looks smaller than our barn," Caroline said, swallowing hard.

"We lived in the barn before Father and Mr. Ben built us the frame house," Martha said matter-of-factly.

"The trees are so big!" Eliza cried.

The trees surrounding the log cabin were wider than Uncle Elisha and Mr. Carpenter were tall. They grew up and up, towering over the little house.

Just then Uncle Elisha and Mr. Carpenter pulled the wagons into the clearing.

"Shall we go inside?" Mother asked cheerfully.

"I thought I'd never get me an invite," Mr. Carpenter said, laughing. "Now all I need is some young ladies to escort me." He smiled at Caroline and Eliza and offered them each an arm. Caroline couldn't help but laugh. Mr. Carpenter always made things better.

Giggling, Caroline, Martha, and Eliza followed Mother through the door. Once inside, Caroline stood still until her eyes became used to the dim light. She looked around the room slowly.

There was a large fireplace in the center of the big room. A small black kettle hung from an iron crane in the hearth. There was an opening for a window along the back wall. Two oak planks jutted out of one of the side walls. They rested on short split logs, forming a table that reached into the center of the room. Beside the table was a doorway that led to another room.

"Looks like the cabin Father built when we first came to Brookfield," Martha said.

"That cabin had a floor," Mother replied.

Caroline looked down. The dirt floor was damp and muddy from spring rains.

"This cabin will have one, too, Charlotte," Mr. Carpenter promised. "I wouldn't think of leaving you and the children here without one."

"We'll also need to build a good door right away," Uncle Elisha said. "And get some panes for the windows."

Uncle Elisha crossed the room and looked up at the rafters. "Don't forget there's a loft, Charlotte," he said. "Though we'll need to build a ladder to climb up to it."

"Who will sleep up there?" Eliza asked.

"Your brothers, if it's built soundly enough," Mother answered. And then she turned and walked to the other doorway. "The girls and I will sleep in this room."

Caroline peeked into the empty room. A ray of sunlight spilled through a window opening. On the dirt floor in the center of the room was a pool of water.

"Don't worry," Mr. Carpenter said.

"First thing tomorrow we'll build bed frames. Come tomorrow night, you and your sisters will be warm and happy as three bears in the thick of a winter's freeze."

"Yes, sir," Caroline said in a small voice. She could not look up into Mr. Carpenter's face. She had a lump in her throat, remembering her big soft bed at home in Brookfield.

But Caroline did not have time to be sad. Everything became busy at once. Henry and Charlie went off to fetch water from the river nearby. Mr. Carpenter and Uncle Elisha began to unpack Mother's stove.

"A hot meal will boost all our spirits," Mother said cheerfully.

Joseph built a roaring fire in the hearth. Mother mixed fresh corn bread batter and poured it in the kettle above the fire. Then Mother heated the last cans of Boston baked beans.

After supper Uncle Elisha laid a thick blanket in a dry corner of the girls' bedroom. He laid the straw mattress on top.

Caroline helped Eliza into her night clothes and then changed herself. It felt good to wear her soft flannel nightgown again.

As soon as Martha got into bed, she fell into a deep sleep. But Caroline tossed and turned trying to get comfortable. The straw inside the mattress was old and broken, and it couldn't make the hard floor feel anything but hard.

"Do you like it here, Caroline?" Eliza whispered.

Caroline didn't answer. She stared out the dark window, biting her lip.

"I don't," Eliza continued. "I wish . . ."

Her voice quivered, and she stopped speaking as her little body began to shake with sobs.

Caroline wrapped her arms around Eliza and hugged her close.

"It's all right," she whispered. "Uncle Elisha and Mr. Ben will make this house a whole lot better than it is now. And there's so much to explore." Caroline tried

her best to sound excited. "Henry said the river is close by and it's as pretty as any river he's ever seen!"

Eliza's shoulders stopped shaking. After a little while, her breathing became steady. Caroline settled back on her side of the mattress and turned to watch the window again. There were a few stars now twinkling through the small space.

Caroline thought about how Mother and Father had often slept on dirt floors in cabins without windows. They had moved from place to place in the wilderness before Caroline was born.

Closing her eyes, Caroline knew that Mother would make this cabin a home and settle this wilderness, too. As she drifted off to sleep, Caroline promised herself that she would help.

# CHAPTER 7

# Beds and Braids

The next day Mr. Carpenter built two large bed frames, one for the girls and one for Mother. When it was time to lace the beds, he called Caroline and Eliza and Martha into the small bedroom to watch.

Slowly Mr. Carpenter pulled a thick coil of rope up and down the bed frames. Then he went from side to side over the frames. When he was finished, each frame was crosshatched with row after row of little rope squares. He leaned over the beds and pressed firmly on the rope squares with both hands.

"Until I have the time to carve some pegs and finish these beds," he said, "you can walk on these springs whenever they start to sag. Shift 'em around with your feet until the sag is all gone."

"Yes, sir!" Eliza sang out.

"May we try now?" Caroline asked.

"Why not?" Mr. Carpenter laughed. "But be careful."

In their bare feet, Caroline, Martha and Eliza climbed up on the beds and began walking across the rope springs. They carefully stepped from square to square, shifting the ropes until they were straight and tight.

Then they hopped off and pulled the mattress on top of their frame. Caroline smoothed out the bunched-up straw.

 54

Martha spread their thick quilt over it.

"It's perfect, Mr. Ben!" Caroline said happily.

Next they made Mother's bed as well. When they were finished, Mr. Carpenter said that if Mother would let them, they could go out and help their brothers clear away the brush and saplings around the house. Everything had to be cleared before Mr. Carpenter and Uncle Elisha could begin chopping down the big trees and turning the ground over for planting.

At first Mother did not want to let the girls go. She did not think young ladies should do the hard outside work. But there was so much to be done around the little cabin that she finally gave in.

Martha was excited to go outside to be with the boys, but Caroline wasn't so sure.

Henry and Charlie had been clearing away brush all morning. They had come to dinner with their hands aching and their shirts and trousers covered with dirt and leaves. Caroline hated to get her dress dirty. She walked slowly out into the after-noon sunshine, frowning and fingering the folds of her brown wool skirt.

Suddenly Martha stopped in front of Caroline.

 56

"I bet you're thinking about your dress and how dirty it's going to get," she said in a teasing voice. "That's just what you're thinking, Caroline. Say so if it's true!"

Caroline felt mad. She looked at Martha and said, "How do you know what I'm thinking?"

"What does it matter if your clothes are dirty?" Martha asked. "You don't have a school to go to anymore or friends to see in town. No one's going to notice your dress, no matter what it looks like."

"Seems to me you're the one who should want to look nice, Martha, since Charlie's come to stay with us," Caroline snapped back. "Too bad your hair is always a mess, and your face and hands are never clean. If I was Charlie, I wouldn't look at you twice."

The moment the mean words were out

of her mouth, Caroline was sorry. She watched a tear roll down Martha's face and wished she could take it all back.

"I . . . I'm sorry, Martha," Caroline stammered, but Martha had already turned away.

"I'm going to help Mother with supper," Martha whispered. Then she ran back to the log house.

Caroline sighed. She took Eliza's hand and led her through the clearing. The ground was littered with brush and small trees Joseph had cut.

When they found Joseph, he told them to pull as much of the brush as they could into the pile Charlie was making at the edge of the clearing.

"You pull the brush and small things," Caroline told Eliza. "I'll take the trees."

Caroline pushed her sleeves up to her elbows and bent over a fallen pine tree.

She grabbed the small trunk around its sticky base and inched her way backward, pulling the tree with her.

When she finally arrived at the pile, her arms were already tingling and her back ached from walking hunched over.

Charlie was singing as he chopped down small trees near the pile. He smiled at Caroline with sparkling eyes.

"Just what we need! Another helper," he yelled. His face was damp with sweat and streaked with dirt, but he was still handsome. And kind and funny, too. No wonder Martha liked him so much.

Charlie looked around. "And where's Miss Martha?" he asked.

Caroline's cheeks turned pink.

"Martha stayed back at the cabin to help Mother," she answered. "I'm going for more trees."

Charlie nodded and grinned. Then he burst into another song.

Caroline hurried back to the middle of the clearing. Now she was determined to work twice as hard. She would pull trees for herself and for Martha as well.

And so all afternoon Caroline went back and forth across the clearing, dragging tree after tree to the pile. She only stopped to rest a little now and then.

Finally she heard the clanging of a wooden spoon against an iron pot. That meant it was time for supper.

Caroline dropped her last tree and walked slowly back toward the cabin. Her hands were sore and stained with dirt. She rubbed them together and blew gently on her fingers.

"Zooks, Caroline!" Henry called. "You cleared away more trees than Joseph and

I could have together."

Caroline tried to smile, but she was too tired. Her back ached and her legs felt wobbly. As soon as she stepped into the cabin, she looked around for Martha, but she was nowhere to be found.

"Wash up quickly, children," Mother said. "Supper's near ready."

Caroline waited her turn, then dipped her sore hands into the washbasin and soaked them in the warm water.

"Goodness glory, Caroline!" Mother cried. "You are a sight to see."

Caroline looked down at her dress. Her apron was even dirtier than the boys' clothes. Her sleeve was ripped at the shoulder, and her hem hung unevenly where it had been snagged and torn.

"I was trying to help the boys as best I could," Caroline said in a quiet voice. "I forgot all about my dress. But I can help wash it and I'll hem it, too."

Mother knelt down in front of Caroline and gently took her sore hands.

"You should be proud of all your hard work, Caroline," Mother said in a soft voice. "These first weeks will be hard, and we must help each other through them."

Caroline nodded. Then she asked, "Where's Martha?"

"She's resting in the back room," Mother said. "She was complaining of a sick stomach, so I told her to rest. Please go see if she's hungry for supper."

Caroline slowly walked into the back room. Martha was lying on their new bed, facing the wall. Caroline wanted to crawl right onto the mattress and fall asleep at once. But she stood quietly for a moment

 62

and then said, "It's time for supper, Martha."

"I don't want any," Martha replied.

Caroline stood for a moment. Then her words tumbled out.

"Charlie's having supper with us. Seeing how he kept asking why you didn't come help drag the trees, I think you should at least come to supper."

Martha rolled over on her side and looked at Caroline.

"You're a sight!" she cried.

Caroline sat down on the edge of the mattress and looked at her red hands.

"Caroline?" Martha asked. She sat up and reached for the brush that sat on the bureau near the bed. "You make the tightest braids of anybody, except Grandma."

Caroline stood up and took the brush from her sister.

"Two braids?" she asked as she loosened Martha's braids and smoothed out her sister's soft hair.

"One today," Martha answered. "I always wear two."

Caroline twisted and tucked Martha's hair into the tightest, prettiest braid she had ever made. When she was finished, they walked into the other room together. Everyone was already sitting at the table.

Charlie was the first to notice Martha's new hairstyle.

"Look at you, all fixed up for supper," Charlie teased. "Makes me almost want to change into my Sunday clothes."

Martha looked down at her plate. Her cheeks flushed brightly.

"Thank you, Charlie," she said. And she reached beneath the table to give Caroline's fingers a squeeze.

 64

# CHAPTER 8

# Tricks

As the weeks passed, the little cabin in the woods began to seem more like home. The clearing stayed warm and sunny during the day, and blossoms began to bloom along the forest floor.

Soon Caroline was back to doing her favorite chore: caring for the chickens. Uncle Elisha had built a small henhouse, and it was Caroline's job to make sure the hens were safely inside each evening. Each morning she opened the henhouse door to feed the hens and let them strut about among the grass and flowers. Then she would go searching for their eggs.

One morning Caroline found five eggs. She knew Mother would be pleased. She placed each one carefully in her basket and was heading toward the cabin when she saw Mr. Carpenter standing in the yard near a huge tree.

"Good morning, little Brownbraid," he called, his eyes twinkling down at her.

Caroline smiled. She liked when Mr. Carpenter called her by her nickname. It reminded her of Father.

"Good morning, Mr. Ben," Caroline said brightly.

"I'm about to measure this tree to make sure it will clear the cabin when I chop it down," he said. "Want to help?"

"Yes, sir," Caroline answered. She carefully set her basket of eggs near an oak tree. Then she followed Mr. Carpenter, giggling as she tried to match his big steps.

Mr. Carpenter measured the shadow of the tree and made some calculations. Then he told Caroline that the tree indeed would fall short of the cabin. He went to get his ax just as Mother poked her head out the cabin door.

"Caroline?" she asked. "Did you collect the eggs yet?"

"Yes, ma'am," Caroline answered proudly. "I found five." She glanced back toward the place where she had left her basket, but she didn't see it. "I'll bring them inside right away," she promised.

"Fine," Mother said.

Caroline dashed back toward the oak tree.

"I was standing right here when we started measuring," Caroline mumbled to herself. She walked around the tree, looking on the ground.

Suddenly she heard a strange sound.

"O-o-o-wah! O-o-o-wah!"

A loud cackling rippled through the trees. Caroline whirled around, her skin bumping up with prickles.

"Who's there?" she called.

"O-o-o-wah! O-o-o-wah!" the shrill voice bleated again.

Caroline looked up. Was it a bird? A crow, maybe?

Then she heard a pile of dry leaves crackling beneath a heavy footstep.

"Who's there?' she called again.

Suddenly a gray hand shot out from behind the trunk of the tree right in front of Caroline. It was holding Caroline's basket.

"Looking for these?" a low voice

growled. Then a gray face poked out above the hand. A mop of dirty curls topped the face. Two piercing blue eyes surrounded by white rings stared down at Caroline. "O-o-o-wah!"

Caroline stared into the eyes. They looked familiar.

"Those are my eggs," she said as firmly as she could. "Put the basket down."

"Mine!" the voice howled back.

Suddenly Caroline realized the blue eyes were laughing merrily at her.

"Henry!" Caroline cried. "Give me back my eggs!"

Henry laid the basket of eggs on the ground and burst into a fit of laughter. Then Charlie appeared beside Henry. His face, hands, clothes, and hair were all a fuzzy dark gray, too.

"These two bothering you, Caroline?" Mr. Carpenter asked sharply.

Caroline turned to find Mr. Carpenter standing there with his musket resting on the ground beside his leg. She could tell that he was angry.

"No, sir," she quickly answered.

"Stealing a little girl's eggs, howling like wolves, and laughing and cackling," Mr. Carpenter scolded. "Seems to me they're causing all sorts of trouble."

Henry and Charlie stopped laughing and looked at the ground.

"We were dumping the ash from the burning pile into barrels," Henry explained. "That's how we got ourselves all dirty."

"We didn't mean nothing by our fooling," Charlie said.

Mr. Carpenter nodded his head.

"We've an acre of land to seed before the week's end, and not one more minute to waste on tomfoolery. Now back to work, boys."

"Yes, sir," Charlie said. "Sorry," he told Caroline as he dashed off toward the river.

"I'm sorry, too," Henry said, squeezing Caroline's shoulders. "You were real brave."

"Best you get your eggs to your mother," Mr. Carpenter said in a gentler voice.

"Yes, sir," Caroline replied, picking up her basket of eggs. She peeked inside to make sure none were broken, then turned back to Mr. Carpenter. "How did you know I was in trouble, Mr. Ben?"

"Well, I was heading back here when I heard that awful cackling," Mr. Carpenter said. "I got hold of my musket and came to take a look."

Mr. Carpenter put his hand gently on Caroline's shoulder as they walked back toward the cabin. Caroline felt so safe with Mr. Carpenter around. But she knew that in a few days he, Charlie, and Uncle Elisha would be leaving. They had to get back to their families.

"I wish you and Charlie could stay here with us, Mr. Ben," Caroline whispered.

"You'll see me again soon, little one," Mr. Carpenter said warmly. He squeezed her shoulder and sighed. "But how Brookfield will miss the Quiner girls!"

Caroline wanted to tell Mr. Carpenter how much she would miss him and how thankful she was that he and Uncle Elisha had turned the unfinished cabin into a warm, safe house. But her words were suddenly stuck in her throat.

When they reached the cabin door, Caroline set her basket of eggs on the ground and gave her friend a hug. Mr. Carpenter looked down at her and his eyes were shining. She could tell that Mr. Carpenter knew what she couldn't find the words to say.